Andrew Sanders

I Have an Orange Juicy Drink

"Becky, Mum, Big Charlie and Big Kik.
I'd never have got here without you." *Porker*

First published in 2016 by Fat Fox Books Ltd. www.fatfoxbooks.com

ISBN 978-1910884041

Fat Fox and associated logos are trademarks and/or registered trademarks of Fat Fox Books Ltd.

Text and illustrations © Andrew Sanders 2016.
The right of Andrew Sanders to be identified as the author and illustrator of this work has been asserted.

A CIP catalogue record for this book is available from the British Library.
Printed and bound in Slovenia.

Andrew Sanders

I Have an Orange Juicy Drink

Porker & Nibblet   **Kik**   **Mummy**   **Big Charlie**   **Cheddar**   **Mr Octopus**   **Raby**   **Coco**

I have an orange
juicy drink.

It tastes yummy.

So yummy.

So very, very yummy.

A naughty alien tried to take my juicy drink.

**So I squished him with
a garden shed.**

*squish

I still have an orange
juicy drink.

It tastes orangey.

So orangey.

So very, very orangey.

A sneaky elephant tried to
steal my juicy drink.

**So I squished him with
an ocean liner.**

squish

I still have an orange juicy drink.

It tastes tasty.

So tasty.

So very, very tasty.

A terrifying dinosaur tried
to take my juicy drink.

squish

So I squished him
with the moon...

And then I rang his mummy to tell
her what a naughty boy he'd been.

(She was NOT impressed with him).

I still have an orange juicy drink.

It tastes juicy.

So juicy.

So very, very juicy.

My brother asked nicely if he could
have some of my juicy drink.

(My brother always has his pet duck on his head by the way).

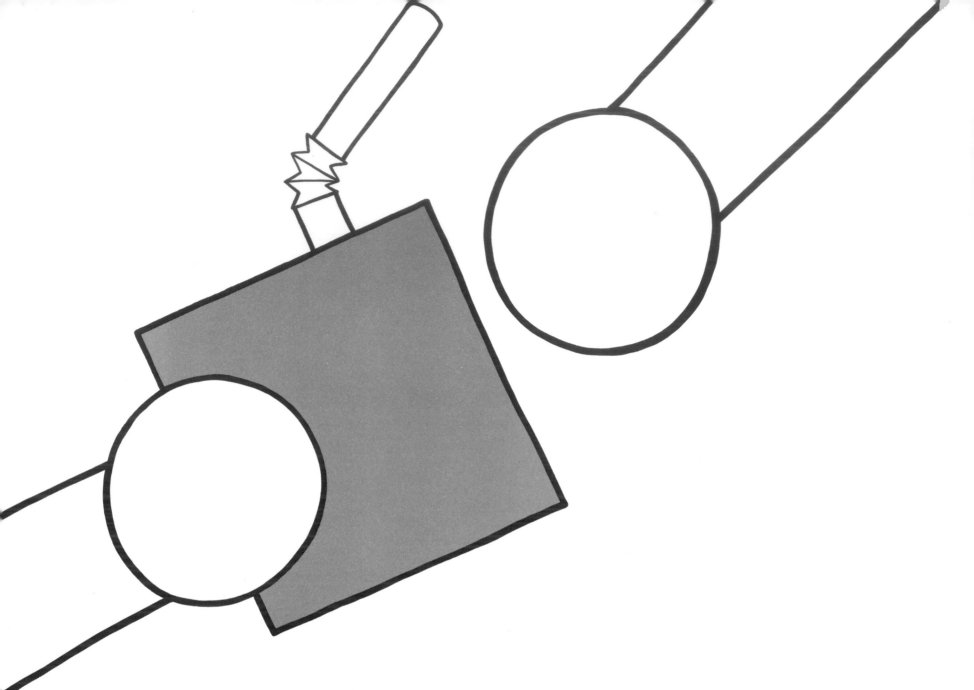

I decided NOT to squish my
brother or his pet duck.

I gave him some of my juicy
drink instead.

I gave him a hug too.

(A good one).

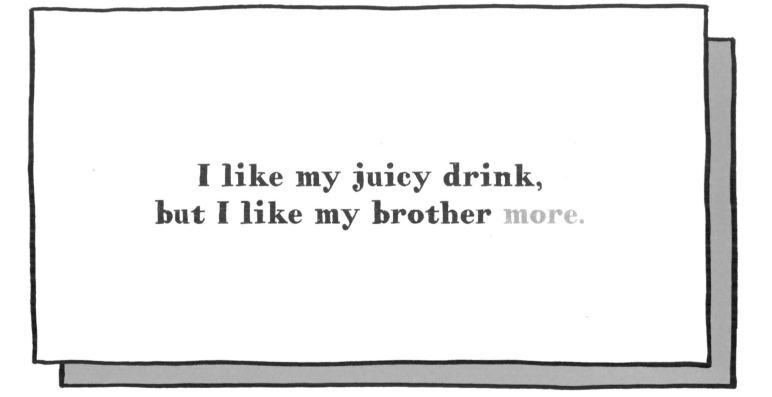

I like my juicy drink,
but I like my brother more.

They learned to ask nicely.